W9-AUZ-298

DR. WONDERFUL AND HER DOG

BLAST OFF
TO THE
MOON!

BY LAUREN GUNDERSON
ILLUSTRATED BY VALERIO FABBRETTI

two lions

One very normal Tuesday, Dr. Wonderful came home from school with two things on her mind:

ONE: Her little dog Newton

TWO: A question she couldn't wait to answer.

Dr. Wonderful loved asking big questions. And answering them felt like solving great mysteries. So she sprang onto her bed, sending Newton for a loop, and asked:

"WHY DOES THE MOON SHRINK?"

"What do you mean the moon shrinks?" Newton asked.

"For the past week I've noticed that the moon is getting smaller," Dr. Wonderful said, pointing to the moon's white crescent. "But a week ago it was getting bigger. Every month it shrinks down to a sliver and disappears before it grows back to a ball. What I don't know is, why?"

The moon is so far away, Dr. Wonderful thought.
How are we going to solve our mystery?

Newton licked her face, trying to be helpful.

Dr. Wonderful's eyes went wide as she got an idea.
"We can go to the moon in the Space-tastic Mind Mobile!"

"I call front seat!" Newton said.

T-minus 5, 4, 3, 2, 1

LIFTOFF!

They soared away from Earth and headed straight for the moon.

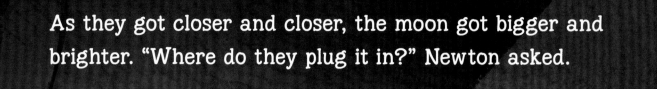

As they got closer and closer, the moon got bigger and brighter. "Where do they plug it in?" Newton asked.

"They don't! But it is bright. I wonder if the moon makes its own light like the sun or reflects light like a mirror?" Dr. Wonderful said.

Then she noticed that the closer their spaceship got to the moon, the larger its shadow became.

"Aha! If we can see our shadow it must mean that the moon doesn't make light like a star. It reflects the light coming from the sun."

"Back on Earth the moon looked like a crescent, but now I can see that the crescent is part of a big ball!" Newton said, getting excited. Anything that looked like a ball reminded him of his favorite game: fetch.

"You're right," Dr. Wonderful said, and started a list of clues that might help her understand why the moon shrinks:
ONE: The moon reflects light.
TWO: From Earth the moon looks like a crescent.
THREE: But the moon is actually a ball.

Newton couldn't resist chasing and chewing his very own ball, which floated around the spaceship weightlessly.

Watching Newton circle around his ball reminded Dr. Wonderful that the moon circles around, or orbits, the earth.

She added to her list of clues:
FOUR: Moon orbits Earth every month.
FIVE: Tell Mom I need a bigger telescope.

Dr. Wonderful did what she always did when she got closer to answering a big question.

"THINK! THINK! THINK!" she said as the spaceship went **SINK** SINK SINK to the surface of the moon.

When they stepped out of their spaceship and looked around at the strange gray ground, all they could say was . . .

"WOOOOOOOW."

Things were very different on the moon than on Earth:
It was so bright Dr. Wonderful had to wear moon-glasses.

And instead of walking, they bounced around like old
balloons. Each step lifted them up higher and set them
down slower than on Earth.

"WAHOO!" Newton said,
jumping off the ground and twirling-twisting-tumbling
before touching back down.

Then they spotted the most amazing thing they'd ever seen: *EARTH*.

They waved to everyone back on their beautiful planet.

During a quick break to play the coolest game of fetch in the universe, Dr. Wonderful noticed that the crescent-shaped shadow on Newton's ball made it look kind of like . . . the moon.

"Interesting," Dr. Wonderful said, pocketing the ball and adding a clue:
SIX: Shadow makes ball look like crescent.

"Come on, Newton," she said. "I think we're close to solving this moon mystery."

As they bounced along, Dr. Wonderful noticed that her shadow was getting longer in front of her as the sun was getting lower behind her.

She added to her list of moon clues:
SEVEN: Shadows lengthen as sun sets behind us.

Then they walked into complete darkness.
The sun couldn't reach them.

It feels like we're in one big shadow,
Dr. Wonderful thought.

She ran back to the bright side of the moon and scribbled down more clues:

EIGHT: The moon has a dark side and a light side.

NINE: Light side is sunny.

TEN: Dark side is in shadow.

"THAT'S IT!" Dr. Wonderful said, standing right in the middle of dark and light.

"The moon doesn't actually shrink. It just looks like it does because of its shadow!"

"How does a shadow make something shrink?" Newton asked.

"Only half of the moon is lit by the sun, while the other part is in shadow," Dr. Wonderful said. "On Earth we can't see the part of the moon in shadow. So as the moon orbits Earth, we see different parts of the shadow, and it looks like the moon is growing and shrinking!"

"Think of the moon as this ball and the sun as my flashlight. If the side of the moon facing you is lit by the sun, you can see the whole bright ball—a full moon. Right?

But if the side of the moon you see is only partly lit by the sun, you'll see only part of the ball, or a crescent!

"And if there is no light on the side of the moon facing Earth, you'll see, well . . . you won't see anything!"

"So the moon is always there even if you can't see it?"
Newton asked.

"Right!" Dr. Wonderful said, and gave Newton a big moon hug.

With their mystery finally solved, they played one last game
of bouncy moon tag before heading home.

That night, as Newton snoozed in the moonlight,
Dr. Wonderful fell asleep thinking, *I wonder
what mystery we'll solve tomorrow. . . .*

THE MOON
is 238,900 miles
from Earth.

THE MOON
is made of rock.

THE MOON
is ¼ as wide as
Earth and you could
fit 64 moons inside
Earth!

CRATERS
are the dents and
dips in the moon made
when meteorites collided
with it long ago.

METEORITES
are rocks flying
through space that
hit the surface of a
planet or a moon.

Dedicated to my curious boys and Henry the dog —L.G.

To Galileo and his telescope —V.F.

Acknowledgments:
Cosmic thanks to the Kennedy Center for commissioning the play, and to Gregg Henry, Kim Peter Kovac, Sean Daniels, Brian Lowdermilk, and Larry Kirshbaum. Special thanks to Dennis Schatz for lending his expertise to the project. —L.G.

Text copyright © 2017 Lauren Gunderson
Illustrations copyright © 2017 Valerio Fabbretti
All rights reserved.

No part of this book may be reproduced, or stored in a retrieval system, or transmitted in any form or by any means, electronic, mechanical, photocopying, recording, or otherwise, without express written permission of the publisher.

Published by Two Lions, New York

www.apub.com

Amazon, the Amazon logo, and Two Lions are trademarks of Amazon.com, Inc., or its affiliates.

ISBN-13: 9781503948372 (hardcover)
ISBN-10: 1503948374 (hardcover)

The illustrations are rendered in digital media.

Book design by Tanya Ross-Hughes
Printed in China

First Edition

10 9 8 7 6 5 4 3 1